Chapter One

It was morning, but Joe was still in bed.
He was playing a game on his tablet.
There was so much brilliant action...

ZAP!

POW!

KA-BOOM!

... he just couldn't tear his eyes away
from the screen.

"Time to get up, Joe!" said Mum. "Hey, why is your room in such a mess?" Mum was right – Joe's toys were scattered everywhere. *That's strange*, he thought.

4

Bolton Council

S

RS

L

UF

BR

Please return/ renew this item
by the last date shown.
Books can also be renewed at
www.bolton.gov.uk/libraries

BLOOMSBURY EDUCATION
Bloomsbury Publishing Plc
50 Bedford Square, London, WC1B 3DP, UK

BLOOMSBURY, BLOOMSBURY EDUCATION and the Diana logo
are trademarks of Bloomsbury Publishing Plc

First published in Great Britain 2019 by Bloomsbury Publishing Plc
Text copyright © Tony Bradman, 2019
Illustrations copyright © Yvonne Campedel, 2019

A catalogue record for this book is available from the British Library

ISBN: PB: 978-1-4729-6342-0; ePDF: 978-1-4729-6343-7; ePub: 978-1-4729-6341-3;
enhanced ePub: 978-1-4729-6957-6

2 4 6 8 10 9 7 5 3 1

Printed and bound in China by Leo Paper Products

To find out more about our authors and books visit www.bloomsbury.com
and sign up for our newsletters

He was pretty sure his room hadn't been
quite so messy when he had gone to bed.
Besides, he didn't play with his toys
much any more – he preferred the
exciting games on his tablet.

"Er... sorry, Mum," Joe said. "I don't know how it could have happened!"
"Is that right?" said Mum. She clearly didn't believe him. "Well, it doesn't matter, seeing as you're going to tidy everything up later after school – aren't you?"

Chapter Two

That afternoon Joe returned Sir Clanky
and the other knights to their castle,
and put Roaring Rita the dinosaur
back on her rock, along with all the
other dinosaurs. He rounded up Eddie
the elephant and Trisha the tiger.

He sorted out his cars and parked them in the right places, and set his train on the railway track. And finally he put his big red plane back together.

For a moment Joe stood there looking at his toys, thinking of the fun he'd had with them in the past. But then he remembered he had a new game on his tablet...

He was still playing on it when Dad
said it was time for bed.

"Night, Joe," said Dad after he'd read
him a story. "Sleep tight."

"Night, Dad," said Joe. He was
yawning, and soon he was falling asleep.

He didn't sleep well, though. He had
a weird dream that his toys came to
life and took over his room. Sir Clanky
stamped around clanking, Rita roared
and Eddie and Trisha chased each
other, trumpeting and growling.

They raced his cars, wrecked his train –
and crashed his big red plane into
his bookshelf!
"Hey, be quiet!" Joe hissed in the
dream. "You'll wake Mum and Dad!"

But the toys laughed and took no notice of him. They got even louder and wilder. Then, suddenly, Joe heard another voice, and felt a hand on his shoulder...

Chapter Three

"Come on, Joe!" said Mum. She sounded rather cross. "It's morning, time to get up – and why have you made such a mess again? It's worse than yesterday."
Joe sat up in his bed and could hardly believe his eyes.

It looked as if a hurricane had blown through his room in the night! Just as before, his toys were scattered everywhere. But now the drawers and cupboards had been emptied too.

His clothes were lying all over the floor, and a pair of his pants dangled from the lampshade.

"Er... sorry, Mum," said Joe. "I really don't know how it happened."

But he was looking at Sir Clanky, Rita, Eddie and Trisha as he said it. He was beginning to think that something rather strange was going on...

Chapter Four

Later, after school, he went straight to his room so that he could tidy up. Mum and Dad helped, especially with his clothes, but it still took ages.

"Right Joe, let's hope the same thing doesn't, er... happen tonight," said Dad, raising an eyebrow. "We'll keep checking on you this evening..."

At bedtime, Mum read Joe a story, then said goodnight. Joe settled down to sleep.

Or at least, that's what he pretended to do. He wanted to find out what was going on, so he was still pretending when Mum and Dad came to check on him.

But it was hard to stay awake as the house grew quiet. He couldn't stop yawning, and his eyelids were growing heavier. Suddenly, Joe heard a noise and his eyes flew open.

He realised several things all at once.
He wasn't in bed any more... he had
shrunk... *and his toys were moving!*

"I knew it!" he said. "I wasn't dreaming
– it was you lot making the mess!"

The toys froze in their tracks, but Joe
could tell they were pretending.
"Don't try and fool me," he said. "It's
way too late for that... I saw you!"
"Oh, all right," said Roaring Rita, and
they relaxed. "You caught us. So what?"

"What do you mean, so what?" Joe spluttered. "I've been getting in trouble with Mum and Dad because of you. Why have you been making my room so untidy?"

"You've forgotten all about us, dear boy, because of that... *thing*," said Sir Clanky. He nodded at the tablet. It seemed huge now Joe was small. "Yeah, you don't play with us any more," said Eddie. "So we're bored."

"And when we're bored," said Trisha, "we're likely to get into mischief."

"Ah, I see," said Joe. "I don't like being bored either."

"Well, would you like to play with us now?" said Rita. "Just for a while?"

Joe looked at their faces, and knew he
couldn't disappoint them.

"Er… OK, why not?" he said. "What
shall we play, then? Any ideas?"

"Oh yes," the toys said together. "We
know how to have fun, don't we?"

Chapter Five

First they played Knights V Dinosaurs, with Sir Clanky and the other knights defending their castle against the dinosaurs, led by Roaring Rita. (Joe joined the dinosaurs' team).

Then they played Dinosaur It, with
Rita chasing and snapping at everyone's
heels. After that they raced the cars,
and then Joe was the driver on the train.
And finally Joe flew them round and
round his room in his big red plane.

"That was great," said Joe at last. "We really must do this again some time." "Whenever you like," said Rita. But suddenly Joe yawned, and felt sleepy…

The next day, Mum and Dad were pleased to see that Joe's room was actually quite tidy.

From then on, Joe did things differently. He still played with his tablet, but he played with Sir Clanky, Roaring Rita and the other toys just as much.
So they all lived happily ever after...

And Joe was much better at getting up
in the mornings!